Dedicated to Kai and Naya - my reason for everything.
And for Harley, Trystin, and Dale.

Special thanks to:
  My extraordinary husband, Ty;
  My favorite critic, DeeDee; and
  My wonderful friend, Andrew.

Braving Bedtime

By Allison Johnson

Love Laugh Read, LLC

Jacob was a strong and brave boy. It's true he was one of
the youngest in his class, but he was already one of the fastest.

He was fast to help out at school

and at home...

(even when the job was a little stinky)

but when the lights went out at bedtime –

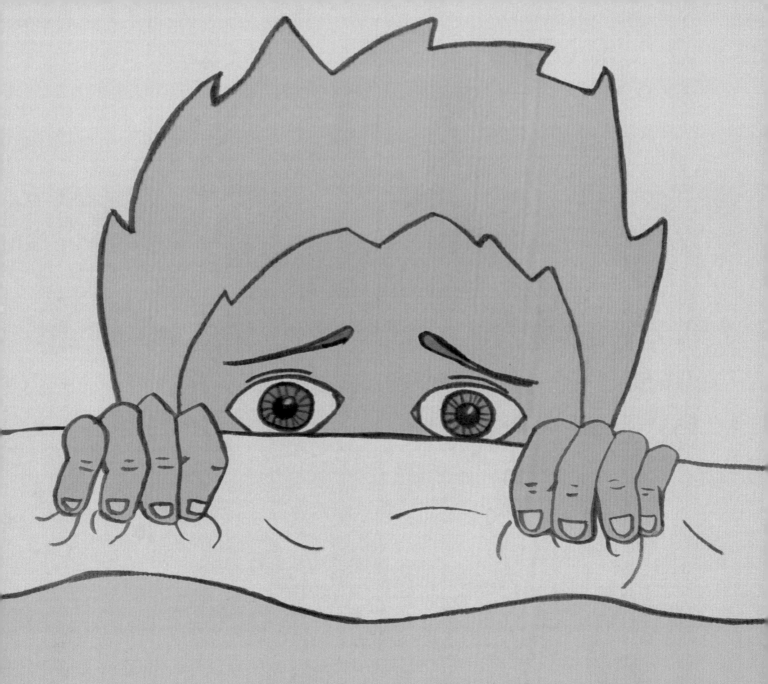

Jacob got scared.

He was sure if the closet door was left open

MONSTERS would run out!

Really mean monsters who would try to eat him

or take his toys

or even worse...

steal his sister!

Jacob tried to be brave. He told himself they were imaginary.
But as soon as he conquered one fear, another sprang up: **shadows.**

He loved his nightlight, but he did **not** love the shadows it made.
He wanted to call out to Mom and Dad, but he knew bedtime was
quiet time. **So** he closed his eyes really tight and finally fell asleep.

In his dreams, Jacob always ran really fast!
But some nights, no matter how fast he ran –
he couldn't outrun the monsters chasing him.

On those nights, Jacob would wake up screaming.
And sometimes even brave boys cry.

When Mom and Dad came in to check on him, Jacob told them all the scary things about bedtime. Mom and Dad knew just what to do.

"You like running, right?" Mom asked. Jacob nodded.
"So run away with your imagination.
Don't let it run away with **you**. You can tell
your imagination what to do. Here, we'll show you."

"Instead of imagining the monsters are coming to eat you –

pretend they're coming to feed you." Mom suggested.

Dad said, "Maybe they're not taking your toys –

maybe they're fixing them."

Mom added, "And did you ever think they might be taking Natalie...

"Monsters aren't always bad, son. Sometimes they're just misunderstood."

Jacob whispered, "What about the scary shadows?"

"You know how we make shapes out of the clouds?" Dad asked.

"Yes but clouds aren't dark and creepy." Jacob answered.
"Shadows don't have to be either. They can be anything
you want them to be. Watch."

Dad turned out the light and shadows raced to the wall.
Jacob hid his face.

"Tell me what you see, son." Dad urged.

"A big mean dog with sharp fangs." Jacob cowered.
"Hmm. Mom, do you see a big mean dog?"

"No. I see a big beautiful dog stretching." Mom smiled.
"Me too," said Dad. Jacob rubbed his eyes.

The dog *was* stretching!

Mom pointed to the hand that was trying to grab Jacob.

"And over there, I see a rainbow
with a dancing leprechaun underneath it."

Jacob blinked in disbelief. "How did you do that?"

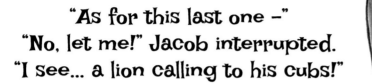

"As for this last one –"
"No, let me!" Jacob interrupted.
"I see... a lion calling to his cubs!"

"He's probably saying it's
time to go to sleep before
we wake your sister."
Dad smiled.

"Wait. I can turn scary things into happy things when I'm awake, but how do I do that in my dreams? I'm asleep."

"Well," Mom said, "when you wake up you can *choose* to be **Brave**." Jacob sighed, "I'm too scared."

"That's what brave means kiddo. Even when you're scared you find a way to keep going." "Even when you're **scared**?! How?"

"First, take a deep breath.
You had a dream someone was chasing you right?"
Jacob nodded.

"What if you were just playing tag?"

"But why did he look so scary?" Jacob asked.
"Maybe it was a Halloween costume." Dad said.
"Does that mean I get a costume, too?" Jacob lit up.
"What would you be?"

"A tiger! No..."

"a pirate!"

"NO!"

"A tiger pirate! *Meow Matey.*"

"Now you've got the idea, kiddo.
What other bad dreams do you have?"

A small voice whispered, "Mommy, sometimes a witch chases me."
Mommy turned and opened her arms. A sleepy-eyed Natalie
climbed into her lap. "Can you show me how to fix bad dreams, too?"
"Absolutely." Mom answered. "What does this witch look like?"

OH!
She is
scary!

"I've got an idea. What if we turned her hat into a giant ice cream cone?" Mom suggested.
"What?!" Jacob laughed.

"Ooh, let's give her jelly beans for eyes!" Daddy said.
"And her mouth could be an orange slice!" Mom added.
"That's silly." Natalie giggled.

"What should her nose be Jake?"

"A carrot!"
Natalie said, "Her ears could be balloons!"

"She'd float away." Dad bobbed his head toward the ceiling.
Jacob folded over with laughter.

Mom said, "A fire breathing dragon

could become a candy breathing dragon."

"Or he could shoot out water like a sprinkler and we'd run through it like this!" Natalie skipped across the room.

Jacob hopped off his dad's lap.
"And if a monster is trying to take me..."

"I'll pretend he's taking me to Jump Palace!"
Jacob jumped around with Natalie.

"Feel better, bud?" Dad asked.
"Lots! Now when I get scared I'll just make it silly."

Natalie leapt into Mommy's lap, "This is fun! Can we do more?"
Mommy laughed, "Sure! Tomorrow. Right now it's bedtime."

Mom and Dad tucked Natalie and Jacob into their beds.
"Good night, kiddos. Sweet dreams."
"You mean silly dreams." Jacob winked.
Dad turned off the light.
"WAIT!"

Jacob hopped out of bed,
opened the closet door, and whispered –

The End

Epilogue

If these sound more like your scary dreams – don't sweat it –
give yourself the giggles.

Is a spider chasing you? What if he's
a tap dancer in need of an audience?

Mummy haunting your dreams?
He might be all wrapped up from
his day at the spa.

Or is a ghost following you?
The reason might be she
needs someone to Waltz with.

Bad guys shooting at you?
Check the bullets.
I'm sure they're marshmallows.

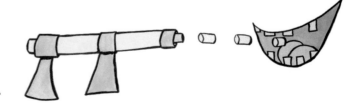

Now silly dreams to all
and to all a sweet night.

Made in the USA
Lexington, KY
19 February 2019